Police
Hurrying! Helping! Saving!

by **Patricia Hubbell**
illustrated by **Viviana Garofoli**

two lions

two lions

Amazon Publishing
Attn: Amazon Children's Publishing
P.O. Box 400818
Las Vegas, NV 89140
www.amazon.com/amazonchildrenspublishing

Library of Congress Cataloging-in-Publication Data
Hubbell, Patricia.
Police : hurrying! helping! saving! / by Patricia Hubbell ; illustrated
by Viviana Garofoli. — 1st edition.
p. cm.
Summary: Illustrations and rhyming text celebrate police officers
and what they do.
ISBN 9781477810668
1. Police—Juvenile fiction. [1. Police—Fiction. 2. Stories in rhyme.]
I. Garofoli, Viviana, ill. II. Title.
PZ8.3.H848Pnp 2007
[E]—dc22
2007030156

The illustrations are rendered in digital art.
Book and cover design by Vera Soki
Editor: Margery Cuyler
Jacket illustrations by Viviana Garofoli

To retired Connecticut state police sergeant Martin A. Ohradan
—*P.H.*

To Emma and Abril
—*V.G.*

Thanks to Lieutenant David J. Dudeck, Jr.,
Princeton Borough Police Department,
Princeton, New Jersey, for his input.

Wooohhh-ahh!
Wooohhh-ahh! Wooohhh-ahh!

Police rush off to start their day.
Who knows what jobs will come their way!

The chief is head of the whole crew.

He checks on what the others do.

Solving crimes both old and new, detectives look for every clue.

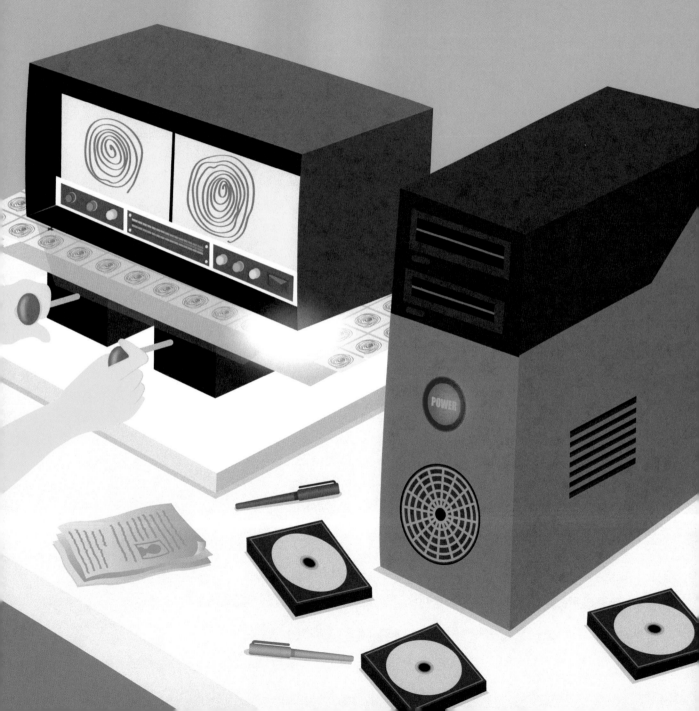

A patrolman walking on his beat chases a burglar up a street.

Police have dogs that search and find.

German shepherds.
Steady. Kind.

**Sometimes police bring dogs to school.
Dogs must obey! That is the rule!**

A policeman's often called a cop.

Some cops ride horses—
clip- clip- clop.

Police tell cars to stop! And go!
Tell speeding drivers to go slow.

They give directions. Give first aid.
They join parades. Lead motorcades.

Police help kids to cross a street.
Their gloved hands wave.
Their whistles tweet.

Police ride bikes.
They ride in cars.
Their shiny badges
glow like stars.

Sirens wail. Wooohhh-ahh-wooohhh!
Bright lights flash. Coming through!

Motorcycles swerve and vroom.

Police ride fast!

Brroom! Brroom! Brroom!

In boats that buck and zoom and roar,
police patrol along the shore.

**When flames flare high
and smoke blows black,
police keep people safely back.**

Wooohhh-ahh! Woohhh-ahh!
Wooohhh-ahh!

NYZ 103

Police work hard to make things right.
Who knows what jobs they'll do tonight?

Patricia Hubbell lives in Easton, Connecticut. She has written many poetry books for children. You can visit her on the Web at www.kidspoet.com.

Viviana Garofoli was born in Buenos Aires, Argentina, where she lives now with her husband and two daughters. She has illustrated more than twenty children's books.

Patricia Hubbell and Viviana Garofoli also collaborated on *Firefighters: Speeding! Spraying! Saving!*, about which reviewers have said the following:

"Preschoolers will point at the bright pictures and act out the urgent, noisy rescue drama in this simple story."
—*Booklist*

"This attractive book on a popular topic will be a big hit at storytime and perfect for one-on-one sharing."
—*School Library Journal*

Made in the USA
Coppell, TX
19 April 2022

76812300R00021